A bug's life

The Quest for the

One Big Thing

story *by* Lou Fancher
paintings *by* Steve Johnson *and* Lou Fancher

Disney PRESS

NEW YORK

In late summer, Princess Dot waited eagerly for the circus bugs to return to the ant colony for the harvest. Each day, she woke up early and ran outside to look for her friends. Finally, Dot checked the calendar and realized that the twelve days of the harvest began the next day!

In the morning, although she was not sure how much harvesting **1** ant could do, Princess Dot set out alone. A delicious smell, a mouthwatering, yummy-yummy smell, floated through the air. Dot climbed up on a blade of grass. Suddenly, a dewdrop knocked her over and she tumbled and toppled and landed on an enormous pillowy sticky . . . thing.

Dot licked sweet goo off her legs and smiled. This was going to be a great harvest—if she could just get this One Big Thing back to the colony. Dot tried to lift it, but it was too big. Determined to begin the harvest, she gathered **12** grains of pollen from a nearby flower and hurried home.

The next day, Dot told her sister, Queen Atta, about the One Big Sticky Thing and how it must have her royal attention. The **2** ants set off.

The One Big Thing looked even bigger and stickier today. They tried to lift it, then to push it, but it would not budge. Instead, Dot and Atta found **11** dandelion seeds curled in a leaf, and carried them back to the anthill.

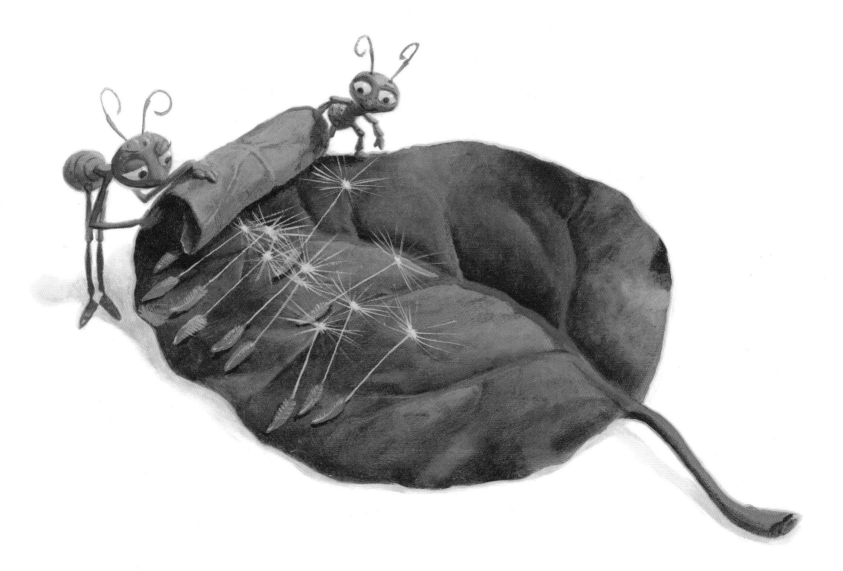

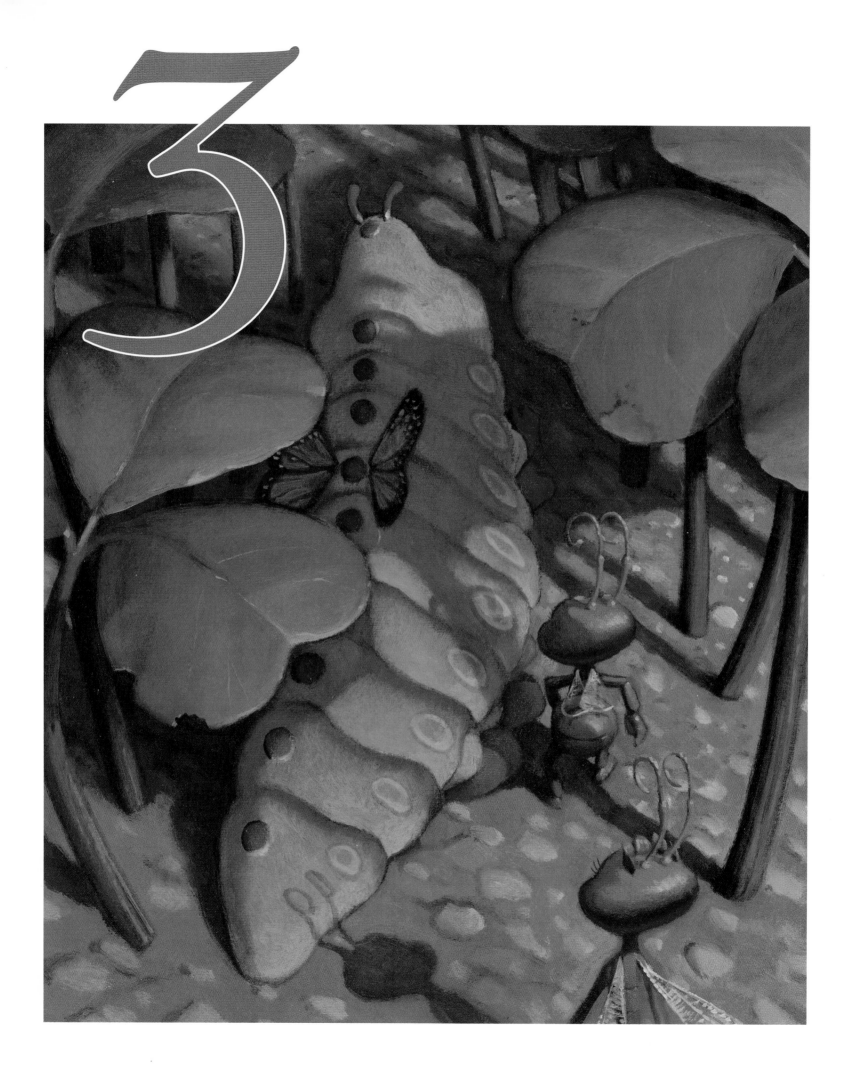

On the third day of the harvest, Heimlich arrived. The rest of the circus bugs had stopped for the night, but Heimlich was too hungry and excited to sleep. He ADORED food, he LOVED the harvest. When Princess Dot described the One Big Gooey Thing, he insisted the 3 of them depart at once.

They tried to pull it, but it would not move. Heimlich pointed out that the One Big Thing was truly gooey and big and perhaps if he were to *eat* half of it first, they might be able to move it! Dot knew where this was headed. Instead, she plucked 10 moss stars from a pebble to take back for the harvest.

On the fourth day, the rest of the circus bugs arrived. Dot was sure that 4 of them would be just enough to get the One Big Sweet Thing. They asked Gypsy to join them and snuck out while everyone else was napping.

Dot pushed while the others pulled—until Gypsy suggested trying one of Manny's magnificent transformation tricks. She flapped and chanted and twirled around, but the One Big Sweet Thing just sat there looking stickier and gooier. Discouraged, they headed home, dragging 9 slender stalks of wheat through the grass.

The harvest was now in earnest. Slim, who had overheard Heimlich talking in his sleep about a tasty gooey secret, offered to help. Dot told him the whole story, and the 5 of them left the colony.

When Slim saw the One Big Thing, he pointed out that it was actually One Big *Twisty* Thing. And the very best way to move anything twisty was to roll it. They tried for hours, but eventually settled for rolling 8 flowers filled with nectar back to the anthill.

On the sixth day of the harvest, Dot decided they needed a real magician on the harvest team. She found Manny. Although he had never levitated a Big Twisty Thing, he agreed to try, and the 6 harvesters departed.

Shouts of "Hocus-pocus" and "Abracadabra" did not move it. Miracle dust and powerful powders floating in the air could not even budge it. They leaned against the One Big Thing and watched 7 buttercup petals fall to the ground. Dot gathered them up to bring home.

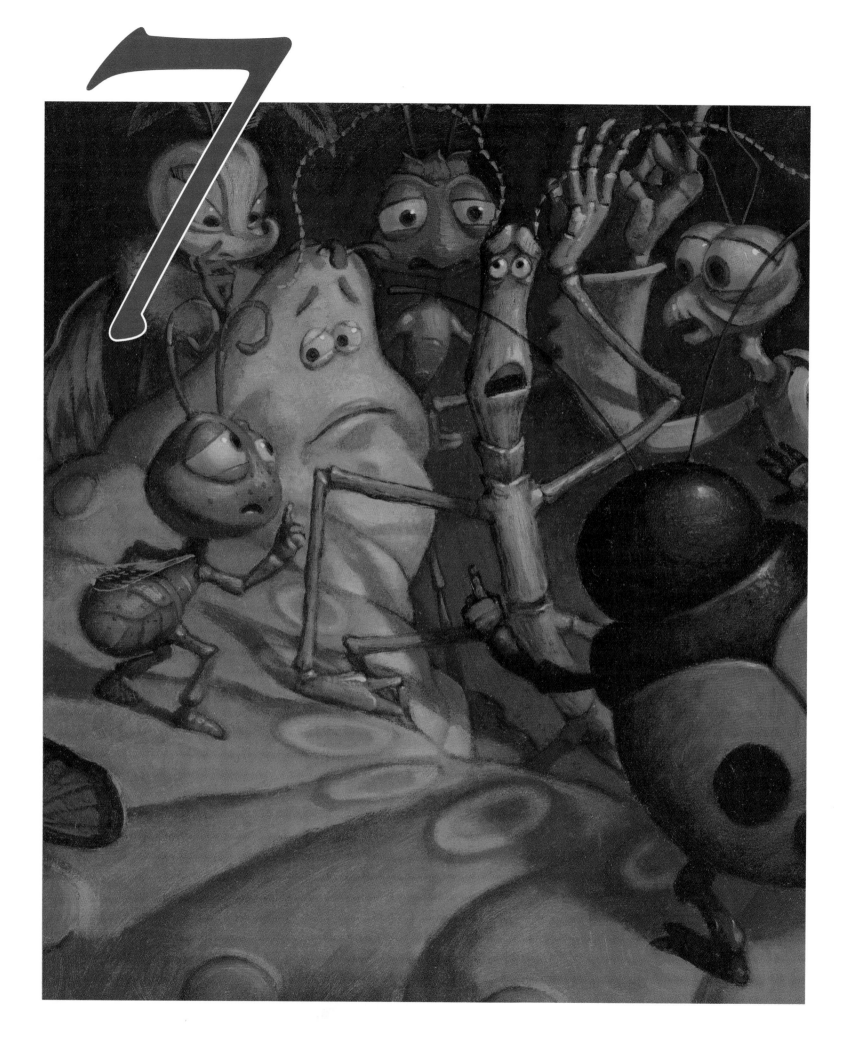

The next morning, Queen Atta called a meeting to tell everyone about the One Big Thing. Manny had a new plan. Slim wanted to drop the whole thing. Pretty soon all of the bugs and ants were buzzing and talking at the same time. Flik emerged from his lab and quieted everyone. He suggested that 7 harvesters try, and waved as they headed off.

Once there, Francis got into a sticky fistfight with a hungry group of flies. Protecting the One Big Thing used up everyone's energy. After chasing the flies off the island, the weary bugs collected 6 tiny blueberries for the harvest.

On the eighth day, Dot *almost* gave up. She was tired of tugging and pushing and twisting. But Dim flexed his mighty wings and said the One Big Tasty Thing wasn't too big or too tasty for him! So the 8 harvesters set out.

When they reached the One Big Thing, Dim pushed while everyone pulled. They worked until they were exhausted. Finally, they stripped 5 pieces of bark from a tree . . . but they all knew that bark strips were not big or tasty or even sticky.

On the ninth day, Rosie could not bear looking at their glum faces and droopy wings. She cracked her silk whip in the air and marched **9** of them straight to the One Big Honey–Glazed Thing.

This time, they lifted it off the ground and began to inch forward. Honey–glazed goo ran down their legs. Blades of grass twisted around their ankles until they collapsed in a snarl. No one was hurt, but even the **4** crab apples they found did not smell as good as the One Big Thing.

The next morning, the colony was a quiet, dreary place. When Dot suggested that 10 harvesters might be exactly the right number, Atta just rolled her eyes. Even Tuck and Roll's comic imitation of Hopper could not cheer them up.

With only two days left for harvesting, Dot wondered if they would ever get the One Big Thing. She watched 3 raindrops splash into a nearby acorn cup and tried to think of a plan.

On the eleventh day of the harvest, Dot made an announcement. She was going to make a final attempt to get the One Big Thing. Anyone wanting to be *truly helpful,* anyone wanting to eat delicious, mouthwatering, yummy–yummy food instead of bark, could come, too. **11** harvesters marched out of the colony together.

With spider silk and acorn cups and even a bit of magic, they managed to prop the One Big Thing on its end. Unfortunately, no one could agree on what to do next and taking a vote was clearly impossible. Too tired to go back to the colony, they curled up under **2** leaves and fell asleep.

Meanwhile, back at the colony, Flik finished a new invention. He rushed out of the lab shouting for everyone to come and see his creation. The colony was empty, completely silent.

Outside, he discovered a well-worn path leading away from the anthill, and set out.

Flik found his friends sleeping near an enormously tall . . . Thing. He woke them up to describe his invention. He wiggled his legs like mechanical arms, grabbed the spider—silk ropes, and backed up right into the One Big Thing!

Flik bumped it hard enough to send it careening end over sticky end down the hill. It catapulted off a rock, flew high in the air, and disappeared from sight. All 12 of them chased after it.

The One Big Thing made a sticky, gooey, honey-glazed landing right outside the colony entrance. There was more than enough food for the winter. And there was even dessert!

Dot knew she would always remember this harvest because everyone worked together to get the **One Big Thing**.

ISBN: 0-7868-3198-7 (trade).